Being Different

by

Carl L. Smith

RoseDog✿Books

PITTSBURGH, PENNSYLVANIA 15222

RoseDog Books
701 Smithfield Street
Pittsburgh, PA 15222
Visit our website at *www.rosedogbookstore.com*

ISBN: 978-1-4349-3100-9
eISBN: 978-1-4349-7168-5

Being Different

By Carl L. Smith

(M)

Part 1: Childhood

This has to do with true things over children when they first start something on their own in school. Will they fit in with other kids and will they be ok? This story also has to do with the issues that we hear and see over kids, what they're thinking? And what thoughts they have on what to do to this person. The word different will show and tell the things people should not do for a person to go bad...

1

In a small town in Texas, a small boy name Christopher was different from any other kid. His face had freckles, a big nose, puffy eyebrows, and a shaved head. He also had a little stuttering when he spoke. He lived with his Aunt and Uncle. He didn't have any friends at all because of being different; no one cared about his feelings.

At the summer of 2001, he was playing outside by himself when he saw some neighbors moving in from across the street. He stopped what he was doing to see who was moving in. His Aunt and Uncle came outside to see the new neighbors as well. They saw a big truck, two cars, and a boat, from what they saw it looked like rich people.

"Just what we need, something to take up half the street." Said Christopher's Uncle

As they went back inside, Christopher saw two kids getting out of the car. One looked like he was twelve and the other one was a girl that's the same age as Christopher (ten).

She looked beautiful, had black hair, blue eyes, medium weight, and had a smile like an angel. When she got out, she looked at Christopher from across the street smiling at him and waving. Christopher got up from playing and ran inside over being scared.

The girl didn't see anything wrong with her smiling, but what she was thinking was maybe the boy was just shy or just never met a girl before whatever the reason, she wanted to meet him at some point.

In the house, Christopher was in his room drawing monsters or animals. And while in his room he heard the news, "A special news report, a shooting at a school happened today. A kid came to school with a gun and shot up some of his classmates. No one knows the reason why it happened; it just became a terrifying issue."

When Christopher's Aunt and Uncle heard about it his Uncle said, "There's always something going on with schools. No one wants to get involved in helping a child."

His Aunt wanted him to come here for a moment. As he came his Aunt asked him if he is ready for school to start.

"N-N-No I'm not. I have no friends for me to go back to school for."

"There will be new kids in school that you'll meet including the kids from across the street. You may also have a girlfriend as well."

"Now Christopher don't let some kids get to you. If they're giving you troubles go to the teacher.

"Ok-k-k..."

His eyes couldn't tell them everything that the kids did to him and the teachers seeing it, but not doing a thing about it. As he tries to ignore, more things of him get picked on. As he walked off only a tear rolled down his cheek filled with sadness and pain. The things he want good out of life just for him to be ok in the world.

At night time right around nine o'clock, Christopher looked out the window beside his bed at the stars, the moon and the clouds around it.

The girl from across the street was looking at the same thing as well, but also had a journal in her hand using the moon as light to see. Her journal had to do with her day of moving in a new town and seeing a boy that looked shy. Nothing looked wrong with him just seems he needs a friend and just maybe a girlfriend.

2

The next day (signing up for school) Christopher and his Aunt went to the store to pick up the rest of his school supplies. In the store, Christopher ran in to some bullies from last year. One bullies name was Carlos. When Carlos saw him, he walked up to him.

"Hello Christy. Getting ready for school?" ·

"…Yes"

"Yes? Or is it y-y-yes."

Christopher just stood there having his fist clenched up, but then his mom came a long and took Carlos away. Christopher's Aunt saw what was going on and looked at her cart, "Why can't Christopher do something when he's being picked on? This is just not fair to him, for him to go on in life with these things.

As they walked on in the store, they ran into the new neighbors from across the street. Christopher's Aunt walked up to them saying hello and Christopher saw the girl smiling at him again. As he walked to the pet section, the girl followed him while her mom was starting to talk to his Aunt.

Christopher walks to the fish tanks looking at the fish, but little did he know the girl was still following him. In the tank he watched a fish eating a corps of a fish.

"I see you like fish."

Christopher looked behind him seeing her with him and walking to him.

"Do you talk?"

No words for a moment fearing she might say something about the way he talks.

"I'm not going to say anything bad about you. To be honest I see nothing wrong with you... What's your name?"

Christopher looked up at her seeing how pretty she is up close.

"Christopher, w-w-what's yours?"

"Zoiy; your name sounds nice."

"So does yours."

Telling each other their likes and dislikes, for the first time he ever had someone that wanted to have a conversation with him, then her mom came looking for her telling her to come along. So did Christopher's Aunt looking at him smiling. As they walked off, Zoiy and Christopher looked at each other and waved good-bye.

"Looks like you made a new friend."

"Y-y-yes..."

"Now Christopher there's no need for you to be sad, you should be happy."

"I'm just worried.

"About what?"

"If I'll be friends with her still if she moves again."

"It all depends on you if you and she will still be friends for years to come."

Back at the house, Christopher and his Aunt unpacked a few things and got some of Christopher's school supplies set for the next two days. Christopher opened a package of scissors and looked at them. As he looked at them voices came to him a long with laughing as well, "Hey loser, how are you? Oops looks like you dropped your lunch HA HA."

He opened the nose of the scissors putting his fingers between it and crying briefly as he slowly closed them. His Aunt saw what he was doing and quickly took them out of his hand telling him not to do that and seeing the same upset look.

A minute later, Zoiy came knocking at the door asking to see if Christopher is willing to come out and play? His Aunt told her to wait as she closed the screen door. Zoiy saw Christopher sitting down with his head down. She stood there and listened to his Aunt talking to him.

"Christopher what ever your doing stop it… Don't let what's ever in your head get to you. There's no need for it."

"All the bullies like to pick on me."

She looked at his hands and as she held on to them, Zoiy saw what she was doing.

"Christopher, don't let bullies get to you. They just do that because they feel sorry for themselves. Just laugh or ignore it, ok?"

"…Ok."

"Now go outside and play with your new friend… Go on."

As he went out the door with Zoiy, she looked at the pictures on the wall. She saw his mom and dad's picture with the three out side together and as she looked out the door said to herself, "I wish ya'll were here… Just to help me with your son. Seeing this happening to him makes me worry about later on when he is grown up."

3

Outside, Christopher and Zoiy didn't go too far because the park was not far from where they lived. They played in the sand making sand castles and covering their hands and popping them out like frogs coming out of the ground, went to slide, and swinging. At the swings, Christopher didn't like to swing at all, but when Zoiy got on the swing he tried it. At first he pulled the chains to get them to move but that didn't work then he watched Zoiy do it by seeing her walking backwards, lifting up her feet off the ground and swinging back and forth. And he did the same thing.

As he swung, he started to like it. Zoiy saw him swinging like crazy along with being happy. She saw the smile on his face and she liked it as she dragged her feet on the ground and looked at him

"… What?"

"Do you like ducks?"

"Yes!"

After she said that; he leaped out of the swing, into the air, and on to the ground.

They walked to the pond and saw the ducks. They saw three kinds a black, white, and a swan. Also some babies going in the water. All but one didn't go in the water because he was different from the others. He was small like a ball from jacks and his feathers were gray as well.

Christopher saw this duck and approached it, it did not run off just stood there looking at him. He put his hand out slowly and the duck come a little bit closer and he was able to hold on to the duck. Zoiy came up to him smiling seeing him holding on to the duck, then Zoiy's big brother came a long telling her to come home.

Her brother walked up to Christopher seeing him holding on to the duck.

"You're taking care of my sister for me?"

"Yes he is, he's also one of our neighbors."

"Is he? I'm Carl; I'm Zoiy's big brother as you can see."

Christopher smiled looking at him, "H-h-h-hello Carl nice to meet you"

"Well we have to go."

As they started to walk off Carlos was not to far away.

He walked up to Christopher from behind with a smirk on his face and looking at the baby duck, "Hi Christy... Nice duck."

He grabbed the duck from him pulling its head off, throwing it, and stomping on it. Christopher watched him do this, Zoiy turned around and saw Carlos messing with him and ran to them. Carl saw this and went with her. She came beside Christopher telling him to go away. He looked at her seeing him having a girlfriend.

"I see you have a girl with you... Shouldn't you be with a boyfriend Christy?"

"Leave him alone! Stop picking on him."

"Why? Its fun."

Carlos kept on going and on until Christopher stood there upset and his mind having voices laughing at him, then he saw him jumping on Carlos hitting and grabbing a rock when that came, Carl came in and he lost the thought.

"You need to stop it or I'll give you a black eye so your friends will laugh at you."

So he did, as he walked off he looked at Christopher telling him to see him later with a smile.

When he left, Zoiy and Carl saw Christopher looking at the baby duck and walking off upset Zoiy told him to wait but he didn't stop he kept on going.

"Please stop Christopher... I want to help you with what you're going through."

Carl grabbed Zoiy to keep her from going after him.

"Let go of me! Let go!"

Carl turned her to him having her look at him.

"You can't help him that easy sis if it was easy then his family would have just helped him... From what I'm seeing, he needs more then just help. He needs someone to love."

"I am doing that!"

"But are you seeing what he's going through?"

"YES! Yes... I know what he's been through but only half."

"Then try to be with him so you'll under stand some more."

She held on to her brother crying as she lessoned to her bother over him.

4

Checking in for the school year for elementary, Zoiy was with her mom to be signed in and meeting her new teacher. She also looked to see if Christopher was around.

"His Aunt will be here next for him Zoiy." Said the teacher

"How do you know?"

The teacher smiled she has known him since he was three years old. She comes on some days to talk to his Aunt or him. She's the only person that cared for him in school everyone else didn't want anything to do with him not even other teachers. Zoiy heard this and knew another thing about him; no one wants to be a friend of his, she couldn't understand why? Then Christopher's Aunt and he came through the door. Zoiy saw them through the window and went out of the room to go see them.

"Hey... Are you ok? What happened today was-"

"I don't like talking about it."

The teacher came to Christopher to take him to go sign up for school. Zoiy looked at his Aunt asking her a question on what is going on with him? She looked at her told her the story, "When he was three years old, he was in the car with his parents going to the store, later they were in a accident, and his mom and dad died. Christopher had a head injury from that accident, it's the reason he talks and act."

When she heard this, she thought back on what had happened to him today when the boy messed with him, but all she can do is to help him a little and be his friend.

At Zoiy's home, she wrote in her diary talking about today and what she may have seen out of Christopher:

The thing that I saw out of Christopher was unknown. He had pain and sadness that might of had him feel angry. I do not know but I have to see what else is going on with this issue I hope it won't be too late.

Aug. 9, 2001

Her big brother came in her room to talk to her while sitting on her bed, "Hey, are you doing ok?"

"Yes… Well not really."

"Does it have to do with what went on over Christopher?"

"Yes."

"Well here, maybe this will help."

He put out his hand and opened it up. What he had was a ring that's silver and has hearts and roses around it. Zoiy saw this ring and told him it's his ring, he found it on the ground near a sewer drain. He told her she needs it more then he does and it might bring her luck.

Carl put it in her hand and she put it on. She looked at it and saw a small word on it inside, "Love." Before he went out of the room he told her an important sentence, "Different is a special thing and if you see it and under stand it, you will enjoy it. And that's what I see out of you Zoiy you care for this person just because he's different."

As he closed the door behind him, she thought for a moment and looked at the ring as well then she turned off the light going to sleep.

5

Today was the first day of school just about everyone showed up for being in Jr. High school. Christopher and Zoiy got off the bus together went to the cafeteria to sit down and wait for the bell to ring for school to start.

When Christopher came in with Zoiy everyone stopped what they were doing and looked at Christopher as he walked by. The kids looked at him for so long they called him a freak and worried, then the bully came up to them seeing them together.

"Look everyone the freak has a girlfriend."

"You have a girlfriend?" said a girl, "What for? Maybe she feels sorry for you."

"Or maybe she likes small pinusess."

The principle came a long and smacked the boy upside the head for saying it.

"What gave you the nerve to say that?"

"Sir I didn't mean too—"

He smacked him up side the head again, "Excuse me? You just gave your self a week of detention… No two weeks…Anyone else wants to join him?"

The bell ring and everyone walked off. The principle looked at Christopher and Zoiy, "Are you ok?"

"Yes."

"What about your friend?"

"Yes I'm Ok-k-k-k."

The principle said, "Ok." And told them he'll be around if they need him and let them go to their class.

Christopher and Zoiy went in their classroom to take a seat. Christopher looked at some of the kids seeing them staring at him with a normal look or just looked away looking at the person beside them. He looked at Zoiy seeing what was going on she smiled at him showing him it's going to be ok, the English teacher came in the class told them to get some notebook paper out and a pencil.

"Ok class, today we're going to talk about our summer break."

Everyone rolled their eyes saying o'brother to themselves, but Christopher and Zoiy didn't do that, they just sat there.

"You're going to write what you did, what you liked about it, and it's going to be 800 words and if you do less you will get an F instead of a C or B. And to make sure you all do it, it will be due tomorrow. Any questions?"

They looked at their paper and got started. The teacher walked out of the classroom for a moment one kid stopped writing and walked up to Christopher taking his notebook from underneath him waving it around.

"Hey g-g-give it back to m-m-me!"

"Ok, here."

He threw it to a kid and she threw it to another kid and another and another until just about every kid got involved. Zoiy saw how upset he got along with holding to his pencil and putting presser on the tip of it with his thumb piercing it. The teacher came in the middle of it, grabbed a ruler and slammed it on the desk yelling at them.

"WHAT IN THE WORLD—"

She looked at Christopher seeing blood dripping from his thumb Zoiy saw it too with his face upset and angry not crying in pain with the pencil still in his thumb.

Outside of the nurse office, Zoiy waited to see if he was alright. Along with her writing in her diary as well. The principle walked in the halls seeing Zoiy out in the hall. He walked to her to see what happened.

He took a seat beside her and told her what he had heard, "Some kid were messing with your friend some more did they?"

She stopped writing and closed her diary putting the pencil down on top of it.

"You know have a friend you need to help stop the things that happened to them."

"But what I'm seeing has to do with something else and the kids are triggering the issue."

"So you're just watching when he's being picked on? That's not a very good friend."

She explained over what she has seen over the past couple of days seeing him just standing there with an upset look clinching his fist. While the principle heard this he tried to talk to her again.

"It sounds to me that he sounds loony. And he needs to have more then a friend, people think there's nothing left for them in the world they want more out of it beside a friend. They want someone to love."

In the nurse's office, Christopher set down playing with the bandage on his thumb. Zoiy came into the room to see how he was feeling. She sat beside of him seeing him upset and angry.

"Christopher don't be like this, people like that just need to grow up."

"People like them don't deserve to live. They think the only way to enjoy life is to make someone feel miserable."

She looked at him, grabbed his wrist, and looked up turning his head to her, "What do you mean?"

Then the nurse entered the room telling them to go back to class. As they went out, Zoiy stayed behind. The nurse came up talking to her, "He's lucky to have a friend like you. I hope you're able to help him as much as you can."

"His parents should be the ones helping him not me I'm just his friend."

"A good friend… Parents aren't always around when they're in trouble, but a friend is always there helping, caring, protecting, and understanding. Now parents do the same thing too don't get me wrong, but a friend sees what goes on more then parents do.

Hearing what she said that's all she can do just to help him and be there for him where he needs it the most.

6

After school, Zoiy was not going to walk with Christopher she went with her mom to an appointment instead.

"Are you going to be fine walking home by yourself?"

"… Yes." In a sad look, looking down at the ground wanting her to come.

"Hey, just give me a call on my mom's phone when you get home so I'll know that you made it ok walking home."

She lifted up his head and kissed him on the cheek.

Carlos saw Zoiy not walking with him it gave him the chance to mess with him with out her around. As the car went off, Christopher started walking. Zoiy looked at the mirror seeing him still looking at the ground.

A few blocks away from the school, Christopher walked past the park and there was Carlos laying against a dinosaur made out of poles and pieces of tin. Christopher saw him ignoring him, but he walked up to him.

"Hey loser, why don't you face me by yourself? Can't do anything without that girl huh? She's around you because she feels sorry for you."

He pulled Christopher's bag off of him getting him to listen to him.

"Hey! Did you hear what I said?"

"Look just l-l-leave me along."

"Or what? What are you going to do about it?"

Christopher's mind went to unpleasant thoughts of killing him.

"Hey! Or what?"

He pushed him and Christopher punched him in the face. Carlos pushed him down punching him as well. Christopher got his feet underneath pushing him off and getting on him. Carlos put his hand on his face. Christopher grabbed it biting it tearing off the pinky as well. He got him off holding on to the hand that was bitten and screaming in pain as well. Christopher got up looking at him and the bully looked at him seeing an evil look coming from him that meant he wanted to kill him. He tried to get away, but Christopher grabbed one of his legs stepping on the knee making it bend the other way tearing the flesh and showing the bone he screamed some more tell him to please stop.

And then Christopher's Aunt saw what was going on, she got out of the car quickly grabbing Christopher away from him, telling him to get in the car, as she called an ambulance for Carlos as he was still crying and screaming. Christopher looked out seeing him suffering as he was still screaming in pain.

Hours later, Zoiy and her mom came home an hour ago and saw Christopher and his Aunt just now driving up the drive way. Zoiy was going to go over there to go see Christopher, but she saw them taking forever getting out of the car meant something was wrong. Seeing his Aunt now get out of the car but not him she just went inside and him still sitting in the car.

Zoiy walked up to the car, looking at the passenger side, and seeing Christopher looking straight forward and a look between mad and sad on his face and then she saw blood on his clothing.

"What happened to you?!"

"Carlos wouldn't leave me alone... He just kept on picking on me... So I hurt him. To the point he was screaming in pain."

Zoiy heard what he almost did. She grabbed his hand telling him to please don't do something like that ever again. She pulled

Christopher out of the car and took him in the house to get him cleaned up.

In the bathroom Zoiy got in the tub with Christopher to scrub his back while he was still acting the same as he did in the car. He then finally asked her a question, "Why are you doing this with me? I can do this myself."

"This means nothing to me. Me and my brother used to do this when he was my age."

"Well I hate to see you still do this when we're older."

Zoiy laughed but Christopher was still sad and feeling that pain that was giving to him.

Christopher's Aunt heard them while she was making supper, but as she was cooking she still worried about what Christopher did to the boy and maybe just maybe Zoiy can try to protect him more then she can.

Zoiy and Christopher got out of the tub, got dried, and went out. Christopher's Aunt asked Zoiy if she would like to stay for dinner. She said she would love to, just went to go ask her mom if she could.

Around bed time Zoiy wrote in her dairy before she went to sleep. Seeing and thinking what may happen:

This is the day I saw something unpleasant on Christopher. So unpleasant I can't explain. The blood on him was from Carlos, the bully, and from what he told me, was to the point he made the bully suffer in pain. This is something I got to do soon before it goes too far.

Sept. 3, 2001

Later on that night, Christopher was still thinking about the bully and hearing him laughing in the dream. Christopher hit him to get him to shut up but he didn't so he kept on hitting him and hitting him to the point his face was bleeding but still laughing, then Christopher put his thumbs to his eyes pushing them into the back of the sockets. Still no scream but only the laughing and then he heard other people laughing at him. Laughing so much it came together and not so nice laugh. This made him to the point he woke up and was angry and upset and thought the only way to end it all is by killing them.

7

The next day Zoiy got up to get ready for school at 7 o'clock a.m. Carl came to her room to see if she was ready to go. She told him she'll be out, as she got her stuff and diary; thinking if Christopher will do well today.

Carl saw her come out, but he saw a worried look on her face.

"Sis. Are you going to be ok today?"

"Can I tell you something big brother?"

That's when he knew something was wrong after all, then he told her why she doesn't wait until they start walking to school.

On the way to school, she told Carl about Christopher being violent and almost killing a boy yesterday. Carl told her the same thing that the other two adults told her. She was hoping for her brother to tell her something different.

"Well what more do you want?"

"To help him before he tries to kill!"

"Zoiy that is doing something. And the teachers will help him too if it comes to that."

"BUT YOU HAVE NOT SEEN WHAT I SAW FROM HIM... The look he made when he was in the car that look of sad, pain, and misery covered in the madness he seems to have now."

Carl did not listen to her. All he heard was nonsense, nothing but lies from the things that she puts in her diary.

"Ok fine don't believe me, but the teachers will understand."

At school Zoiy told the principle about what's going on with Christopher. He listened but he too did the samething her brother did as well

"But sir he will try to kill who ever picks on him or maybe others!"

"That's enough Zoiy now go to class."

She walked out the door while slamming it. The principle got to the door opening it up quickly telling her, "Just for that, two days of detention." As she walked out, she saw Carlos coming to school late with a knife showing briefly in his pocket. She looked at him when he came in with crunches, a cast on his leg, and a big bandage to cover most of his hand then saw Christopher coming late as well from over sleeping.

Zoiy saw him look at the bully and walked to him slowly, Zoiy grabbed Christopher by the wrist telling him don't. He looked at her saying, "Leave me alone." Just as Zoiy was doing this, the bully turned around and saw him getting away as fast as he could.

"No, I know what you're going to do and I will not let you do it, this is wrong."

"You d-d-don't understand."

"Then let me understand by helping you."

Just then their teacher comes to look for them. Shortly enough the teacher saw them down the hall and went to go get them, "Come on ya'll! Class has already started!"

Christopher pulled his hand, Zoiy let go of him, and he walked off. The teacher saw a little of what was going on and talked to Zoiy.

"Is everything ok?"

"...Yes."

"Are you sure? I thought I saw something wrong."

"No... Nothing is wrong."

Seeing someone really wanting to help but wouldn't take it, as she walked to the class room, she did nothing but keep an eye on Christopher.

At lunch time, Zoiy stayed close by to see if anything was going to happened seeing Christopher being a little bit near the bully (two people behind him).

Christopher looked at the bully more and more with the most disturbing thought he had that anyone could think of over killing a person. As a teacher takes his tray for him, Christopher turned his head slowly at him. Carlos looked back seeing Christopher giving him an unpleasant smile. He looked forward quickly going to his table.

After lunch, he went to the rest room and so did Christopher a minute later. The bully was on the toilet while Christopher waited for him to come out. Carlos saw feet at his door just standing there.

"Hey you're waiting to go? There's another one next to me." But no movement, then he got up pulling his pants and opened the door, "I just got through telling you—"

He saw Christopher with a pair of scissors in his hand; he pulled the door quickly keeping him from killing him. Christopher pulled as well then saw his fingers showing and stabbed them with the scissors. The bully pushed the door knocking him on the ground. He made a run for it but his leg was hurting so bad he couldn't. Christopher grabbed his foot making him fall, stabbed his foot, and twisting it making the ankle bone break. The scream was so loud everyone in the halls heard it.

The bully crawled out of the bathroom as fast as he could with Christopher slowly walking up to him. He was trying to yell for help but Christopher pulled his head back and stabbed his throat with scissors.

No one did a thing, they ran to get away. Zoiy pushed everyone out of the way to get to Christopher before he went any farther.

He looked at the bully seeing him crying and suffering. The bully looked at him as well putting his hand in front of him; he stabbed it putting the scissors through the hand. He couldn't scream but have a low voice. Zoiy got to him just in time to stop him. She ran into him and pushed him into the wall getting him to stop.

"STOP IT! HE LEARNED HIS LESSON! He's sorry as well. There's no need of killing him."

"… People like him need to die. All they do is make fun of others."

Christopher got off the wall and started walking to him again, "Christopher, PLEASE DON'T DO IT!"

She tried to hold him back, but he stabbed her in the arm letting go of him. He got on one knee and stabbed him in the back three times, Carlos tried to get the knife out of his pocket but Christopher turned him around and once in the chest, moving the scissors in his chest tearing up the heart some more until he stopped moving.

After he was done, he looked at Zoiy seeing her bleeding. His face changed from evil to upset seeing that he hurt Zoiy his only friend. She looked at him crying, he stood there with the scissors dripping blood, then he run out of the school. The principle saw Zoiy hurt and ran up to her to keep her arm from bleeding anymore along with calling the ambulance. She looked where Christopher ran out of to get away then closed her eyes passing out.

8

Zoiy woke up in the hospital on a blood transfusion because of losing a lot of blood. Her mom and brother came to see if she was alright; Carl walked fast to see her and when he did, she saw him.

"Big brother."

"Zoiy what happened?"

She looked at her arm upset and terrified then told him what went on along with their mom coming in.

"… Christopher… He didn't mean to… Do… This!" Zoiy put her hand on her forehead crying some more and seeing the killing that he made.

Their mom left the room seeing Carl needing to talk to her alone.

"What did he do?"

"He killed the boy. All because of not leaving him alone I tried to stop him and help him, but I couldn't I was too late."

He took her hand holding it, "… No its not. It's never to late. You know some things about him now what you saw from him was before you met him. Helping him shows how much you care and if he sees that, he may stop."

"But he ran off."

"Then you go find him. He knows he'll be taken away that's why he ran off. He's also upset over what he did to you."

She thought back on the issue seeing his face being evil then changing to upset seeing her arm bleeding, "Yes I do. It changed, he saw what happened to me then he changed."

"Then find him later on."

"Why?"

"Now is not going to work. The adults will be looking for him and you can't go out by yourself."

She didn't like what Carl told her, she really wanted to go out there now to go look for Christopher before things get out of hand.

Days went by, the news talked about the murder that went on at the Jr. High School and a boy still missing. Zoiy kept on looking out her window to see if he is going to come back home anytime. Her mom came through the door asking her if she seen him? She looked at Zoiy with a sad face, "No, I haven't… Sorry."

Zoiy got off the couch looking at the floor upset and scared still thinking of the killing and the look that Christopher made when he did it. Her mom came from behind holding on to her with tears running down her cheek and hyperventilating thinking all of it was her fault. Her mom told her it wasn't her fault this went on before they came along.

In her diary, she wrote more things that went on over looking for Christopher:

This is like a nightmare; it never goes away most of the time. The adults are still looking and the kids are not worried about him being missing. It's now going too far on everyone messing with one another. I need to understand these issues more to help them but most importantly help Christopher I do not know how but I will look for him it may take me years, but I'll do everything to save him and the people around him.

Sept. 11, 2001

Part 2: Adult hood

The things are worse at older age. Fears are terrifying and killing very brutal, the thing we don't want to have in life but some is over a past the reason they have it is to get rid of or kill just because of how their life has been treated.

9

Ten years later, everyone gave up on looking for Christopher now there are unknown murders going on at this time. Zoiy was all grown up as a detective for Wichita Falls with her hair still black but back, black pants, a plain red shirt, and black shoes.

Zoiy did most of the unknown murders to see what she can find out of them. All the photos she looked at were very brutal, a victim had his eyes gouged out and another one was hanging with his insides hanging out of his stomach.

"They have to be from him, but could he be near by?"

She kept on looking hoping to find something, then she saw a notebook with bloody hand prints on it. She asked one of the FBI if they know anything about the notebook?

"Sorry Zoiy, we looked in it when we saw blood on it and there was nothing written in it."

"Pages were torn out of it. Were there any tears in the notebook?"

"No."

"How many pages were in it?"

They had a strange look on their face not seeing the point out of it. As she told them a notebook has fifty to sixty pages in it for it being thick.

They went to the storage for the cases to look for the notebook. They found the box of the murder of 2010. Zoiy opened the box and found the notebook looking in it. As she looked through the pages, she saw a brief scrape of blood on one page showing it to them.

"See. Blood on a page that means there are pages missing out of it, he took it."

"Who took it?"

"Christopher."

"Would you stop assuming it's that person! That person has been missing for many years now."

"The murders were made by a person that makes them suffer and kills them, that's the only person that does that."

He just looked at her hoping she's wrong still looking for him.

A man miles away got off his job from the base, walking. Another man was in a car looking at him watching him walking home. As he fixed his mirror showing his right eye and waiting to go on a green light. He drove up to him asking if he wanted a ride to his house, but kept on walking telling him he's fine. Then clouds began building up; the man decided to take the offer and got in the car.

As he did, the driver did not look at him.

"Thanks man. Work is sorry, to many retards it would be nice if there were no special people in this world they all should die... What do you think?"

The driver didn't answer and kept on driving. He drove past his home with out stopping.

"Hey you passed it."

Then he stopped the car staying in the middle of the road.

"Hey, are you going turn around?"

The locks locked and the driver slowly turned his head to him.

"Hey man what is this?"

"People like you should not live if you talk bad about others that are different."

The man at the passenger side got scared and tried to get out of the car, then the driver took out his knife, flipped it open, and stabbed him in the leg and dragged it down to his knee twisting the knife and making his knee cap pop off. He tried to fight, the more he did the more he made him suffer, then he stuck the knife in his eyes cutting them up and finished him by stabbing him in the head. He pulled his knife out, got out of the car, and walked off away from the car. As he did, he looked at the knife as it had left over blood on it seeing the person that he hurt he didn't want to hurt and seeing the only friend he had he killed.

10

"Come on Christopher. I still want to help you." Zoiy was still looking at the old files and found nothing else, putting down the file rubbing her right eye and cheek. The phone rang, Zoiy picked it up and heard Frank on the other line telling her there's another murder about ten blocks away from the base in a car.

The rain didn't give them much to find (most of it was washed away). Zoiy looked at the body seeing the same thing, but worse.

"It's the same person. He was very angry at this person."

"What makes you say that?" Frank walked up to the car seeing it as well, "O'gezz! It's like he's been tortured!"

Zoiy looked inside the car looking at the floor board of the passenger side and saw the knee cap at his feet.

"Nothing to fin—" Across the street in a group of trees, she saw someone looking at her with a sad face. She looked a little closer then whispered to herself, "Christopher?" As he went away, Zoiy went around the car walking straight to the other side.

"Zoiy what are you doing?" Frank's talk did not faze her and she kept on going. A trucker stopped and she stopped as well hearing the horn scaring her.

"Hey watch where you're going!"

Frank ran up to her asking her what was she thinking? She looked again knowing she already lost him.

"What? What did you see?"

She stayed quiet for a moment, then told him, "It was nothing. I'm just seeing things." Keeping what she saw to herself, "At least I know he's here."

In an old abandoned factory, almost outside of town, Christopher lives in it and everything was organized. He had clean clothes, power, a small fridge, bed, pictures, and newspaper articles on a big board. The windows were cover over the seen of power being on, articles had the murders he made, and the shootings at some schools on them. The picture had the victims that he spied on and the crime scene with Zoiy in them.

Christopher took a bath with a hose and got into new clothes afterwards. He sat at his table covered with news paper and photos, cutting the articles out and putting them on the walls. The photos he looked at had Zoiy in them and every picture he looked at of her, a flood of memories came to him. Memories of him and Zoiy; smile and a beautiful face of an anger mixed with the pain of everyone gave him and then the murders came as well throwing the scissors, flipping the table over, picking up the chair, and throwing it as well crying and putting his left hand on his knee. He kept on crying and crying until he got up walking away from the mess and went to sleep.

Zoiy looked at the pictures of the murder today a long with writing in her old diary as well:

These murders aren't helping anyone. I seen him at his own killing zone, he thinks killing is the only way to stop what they had done to him. I don't know what ells to do; I need to do more than just look at dead bodies for a murder...

She turned the radio on to hear some music; the question was not helping her. A song came on that was by Peter Yarrow called, 'Don't Laugh at Me'. Zoiy heard it start, stopped writing for a moment and hear him sing. The song told about being different, being picked on, and being lonely. And also not just disability people like a begger around the corner and a single teenage mother. Zoiy cried as she heard this song hearing how sad it was and the words that she heard in it, 'In God's eyes we're all the same.' Zoiy now sees it's not just disabled its everyone people that see them different mistreating them.

There is a way to help Christopher. Everyone else that has the same problem as both mental and physical. We're all the same and someday we'll all have perfected wings.

Nov. 15, 2011

After writing down the date, a tear landed in her diary. She kept it there not drying it and closing it putting it on the coffee table, put the pen next to it, got up to go take a shower, getting ready for bed.

Her dreams came to her from when she was a kid. First meeting Christopher, playing with him, and falling in love with him. She was chasing him to catch him, then everything went black with Christopher disappearing. She stopped, seeing nothing but pitch black in front of her. At first she thought she woke up then light shined on her like a spot light and her older, still in her clothes from her child hood, hearing some kids picking on someone. Not seeing where; another spot light was seen with some kids surrounding someone picking on him and as the circle broke up, she saw Christopher as a boy on his knees and holding the dead baby duck that was stomped on and its head ripped off. As the bullies fade away, the boy was still there saying to himself, "Why? Why does no one care for me? This world has nothing but madness. No kindness, no niceness, no nothing."

She walked up to him combining the lights looking at him and him looking up at her.

"GO AWAY!"

She was shocked hearing what he said to her.

"You didn't help me then! Why now?!"

She didn't say anything to him seeing nothing but how sad he was. Then it lit up seeing blood all over the place and corpses of the victims looking at him again seeing blood running out of his eyes like tears.

"There's no hope for me... Not any more..."

She woke up looking at her ceiling in the dark saying to her self, "Yes there is Christopher. I want to help. I always wanted to help you, from the moment I first saw you... No need for you or anyone else to be alone."

11

It was a Wednesday cool and cloudy, Zoiy came out of her house seeing Frank at her drive way as she stood at her porch.

She walked the other way, Frank ran after her seeing what she's about to do.

"I'm gonna go look for Christopher. He's here."

Frank grabbed her wrist stopping her, "I know what you're thinking, don't."

She pulled to get him to let go of her.

"I know what I'm doing!"

"He's a killer and he'll kill you too!"

"NO HE WON'T!"

"HOW THE HELL DO YOU KNOW?!

Finally she snapped telling him everything about Christopher telling him the good things, the bad things, and nightmares. From where it all started to what he had become. Frank slowly let go of her wrist hearing those words of pain and misery.

"Ok I'll help you. But everyone is now going to look for him cause you found the killer."

"As long we go get him some help."

She got in his car to go look for him.

The search went on for hours, no sign of him any where. Now she sees more police men out and about looking for him as well.

She thought real hard where he might be at, and then she looked at the old buildings.

"Could a homeless person be in one of those buildings?"

Frank looked at her briefly while he was driving, "Yes, but cops look in them every once in a while."

She told him to stop and let her out.

"What are you doing?!"

"I'm doing this alone."

"But he might kill!"

"He won't... Not if he really wants help."

Frank didn't talk anymore but drove off looking at her in the mirror.

She walked to the biggest building on the street, seeing an opening and a little blood on the side of the opening.

"This must be it." Whispering to herself and walking into the entrance.

She couldn't see anything it was pitch black, then the lights came on seeing pictures and news papers on the walls. She know she's at the right place. Looking around to find him, she came across pictures of her. They had hearts around it and wings of an angel, some of them were also torn, on the floor. Then a begat tipped over, she looked seeing someone hiding.

She didn't walk to it, she just stood there looking at that spot having a normal look on her face and felt a little terrified.

"...Christopher?... Is that you?"

No answer, but then there was a response, "What are you doing here? Do I know you?"

She walked very slowly as she was talking to him, "It's me, Zoiy. The one that tried to help you when you were a kid troubled by other kids in school."

He showed himself and she sees that he hasn't grown much. He still had a freckled face and his hair changed from blond to black and his body was built like a foot ball player. As he looked at her closer, he knew it was her.

"I thought I killed you. You lost a lot of blood."

Zoiy showed him the scar on her arm, "I thought so too, but the doctors came just in time to save me."

As he looked at her, he started walking to her with his hand out putting it to her face feeling her warm and soft skin then more memories came to Christopher. The happy ones with Zoiy, holding on to his hand, playing with her, and always made him smile. He was about to cry feeling all those memories of good things.

Then suddenly a bust at the door, a group of cops run in there to grab him pulling him away from Zoiy.

"You're under arrest for all the grisly murders."

Zoiy run after them trying to get them to let go of him, "No! I'm trying to help him!"

Then she saw Frank standing there with a normal look on his face not doing a thing about it.

"You— you told them where he was."

"It's for his own good. People like him deserve to be in jail or put to death."

Zoiy began to yell at him seeing how heartless he was, "DAMMIT, CAN YOU SEE I'M TRYING TO HELP HIM?!" He didn't say nothing else but standing there looking at her, "…Of course not. You're like everyone else. Not understanding what has happened to him to be this way."

Frank didn't go further, then told her to leave (she was fired from fighting with him).

She walked to the car and as she turned around, she looked at Christopher in the police car and he looked at her as well. As the police car drove off, Zoiy kept on looking at him until she no longer seen the car, as she shed a tear, then went in the car to do some packing.

12

*Z*oiy had the TV on as she was packing still sad and upset. The news came on telling everyone about Detective Zoiy catching the serial killer after spending so many years on it and later on might giving him the death penalty. Zoiy looked at the TV seeing Christopher's mug shot. She sits down on the couch not knowing what else to do for Christopher.

Her cell phone ring on the coffee table seeing Carl, her brother, on it then went ahead to answer it. Her brother called just to see how she was doing? She then told him she found Christopher. Carl was silent then talked to her again.

"How is he?"

Zoiy's voice sound upset with being calm, "Not so good. He got arrested for all these murders that went on around here... And will be given the death penalty."

"Is there anything you can do?"

"No... No there's not I tried. I wish I knew more when we were kids just to help him."

Carl then told her to go to the jail to see him, that's all she can do for Christopher. She shook her head, sliding her fingers through her hair, and sniffing, "Ok big brother I'll try to do that"

"Don't try... Do. You love him so much. Everything you did and thought was all about him. I know you Zoiy, you never like turning your back on anyone or forget about them."

Carl told her he will see her in a few weeks, then hung up. Zoiy put down her phone looking at some pictures that were left on the walls. Pictures of her, her brother, and family, she got up, went to her car, and went to the jail.

In the jail, Christopher looked outside the bars seeing a cop looking at him.

"Don't worry about that guy. He's mean to everyone, he thinks he's better then everyone."

A voice in the jail cell was talking to him. Christopher turned around and seen this scruffy looking man, skinny looking, gray, and in his forties.

"So what are you in for?"

Christopher didn't say anything for a moment then told him, "Killing a lot of people. People that don't deserve to live, being so cruel to one another."

The man looks at him see how much sadness and anger he had. No longer talking to him fearing he might kill him as well.

Christopher looked at the door opened seeing Zoiy coming through it. The guard looked at her telling her, she had five minutes to talk to him. She walked to the bars looking at Christopher and him looking at her.

"What are you doing here?"

"I wanted to see you and talk to you some more, its been years since I seen you."

She put her hand against his face he turned his head away from her.

"Why do you want to see me? I'm different from everyone you know."

"But they're not like you before you became this. You're special and kind when people are kind to you, you just deal with the mean things in life."

He looked at her showing a tear on his left side and wiping it off his cheek, "Love you since the first time I saw you and I always will."

He got closer to her face kissing her feeling her smooth and warm lips. Smiling at him as she was looking like she was about to cry as well. The guard broke them up telling her, her time was up. She looked at him and he looked at her as she walked away.

"I want to see you again."

She stopped not saying a thing fearing more pain to him if she told him what's going to happened to him.

"Just so we can catch up with are relationship."

"I don't know if I will Christopher."

Then she went out. Going to her car, stopped going in the car not in no hurry to start the car staring at the steering wheel, crying some more.

Christopher kept on looking at the door and the guard looking at him.

"You're never going to see her again we'll make sure of that. You're nothing but a loser and a killer."

"What do you know Mr. Big shot?"

The guard walked to the jail cell mouthing him, "You're the one that is going to die for killing all those people. She just came here just to feel sorry for you. No one wants to fall in love with you."

Those same words that were told to him ten years ago made him even angrier the guard got close enough to the bars to where Christopher was able to grab him. He grabbed the guard's head pulling it to the bars, like he was trying to pull his face through. The guard grabbed his wrist trying to get him to let go, but Christopher pulled them in grabbing his shoulder also and making his arms bend back words to where the middle of the arm was showing the bone and veins making him scream bloody murder, grabbed his head again and snapped his neck.

Christopher grabbed the keys to unlock the cell, as he got out, the memories got worse. Laughing got bad and Zoiy's voice getting involved with them. Just like that he got into depression, he run out of there with an upset look.

The cops saw him running to the exit, try to get him he shut the door grabbing a bar to keep the door shut, then continued running.

Zoiy was just a few blocks away, when she heard on the police scanner, "A prisoner had escaped. The suspect is running on foot, is extremely dangerous with or without a weapon."

Zoiy knew who they were talking about, then hit the gas to get to him before they did. When she turned around, she saw Christopher running to one of the tall buildings knowing what he was going to do. She unbuckled her seatbelt, got out of the car, and rushed over there.

Christopher went inside making his way to the top, Zoiy was right behind him trying to call out his name, "Christopher! Christopher! Whatever you're planning on doing don't do it!"

Christopher heard her, but did not listen he made it to the top going through the door outside. The top was almost dark with the sun about to set and the higher altitude made it a little colder. He walked to the edge of the building looking down crying, seeing no point of living if he was going to die anyway. The memories got worse by the minute not wanting to hear the voices of being made fun of.

Zoiy got through the door and stopped seeing him at the edge, "Christopher please don't I'm trying to help you. Don't do this to yourself."

He looked at her having some tears running down his cheeks, "There's no point of me living and I can't do this anymore."

"Yes there is. You have me. I fell in love because of you and you did too seeing someone that didn't judge you. And everything else, I will help you with no matter what it takes."

He shook his head doubting her, "You didn't go look for me when I ran off."

"I WANTED TO, BUT I WAS TOO YOUNG," Crying as she was trying to talk, "I did nothing but think about you, writing down everything about me, you, and your issue that was going on in Jr. High... Don't you see? I did whatever I could to find you. I went to the edge of the earth looking for you... And seeing those tears at the crime since and the torn out pages that meant my searching was over."

"Yes it is..."

Christopher put his foot out and began to lean forward looking at Zoiy one last time. Everything in Zoiy's world went slow as she watched him fall off the edge, running to the edge hoping to grab him, but just like that he landed face first and blood running out of his mouth.

Zoiy looked at his body and turned around sitting like a scared little girl having her knees up to her chin, crying and screaming to where everyone heard it.

Frank and the cops went through the door seeing Zoiy on the ground looking at the ground sniffing and crying. Frank slowly walked up to her trying to help her up, but she refused telling him to go away. He tried again, but this time he spoke to her, "Zoiy look. I didn't know this was going too happened, but he's dead it's over."

Zoiy couldn't say anything, to upset to think, then decided to get up going to the door, down stairs, and out of the building. Frank held on to her till she got to his car, before she did, she watch them putting him in a body bag and said to herself, *Good by... My love*, then took him away.

13

Two weeks later, Zoiy was just about ready to move. She stayed longer for Christopher's funeral, also seeing his Aunt and Uncle not wanting to talk blaming her, 'She's the one that brat Christopher to this!' and telling them this was done by him and him only they didn't help him very well when he was picked on she tried helping him, but she was too late.

Frank came to see if she was still here. She seen him at the door and opened it.

"What do you want?" Saying in a disappointed voice.

"There's reward ceremony for you and a speech also afterwards."

Zoiy turned down what was giving to her for solving the murders. She only cared about Christopher, just went back on putting stuff in the car. Then she thought back on her giving a speech. She put down the box in the car, turned looking at Frank, "A speech?"

"The speech was my idea… It is about the reason why you did this. From what you told me and what I saw. You need to tell this to everyone."

She thought some more, then decided to go, she shut her house door, her car door, and got in Frank's car.

The reward ceremony was taking at a football stadium, about half of the town came to it the rest watched it on the television. Seeing Zoiy everyone cheered feeling no longer scare of coming out of their homes.

As she came up to the middle of the field, the reward was given to her. She didn't grab it also shaking her head. Everyone saw her turn it down and started to boo at her, then she saw her brother, mom, and dad coming to the field. Her brother walked up to the microphone telling everyone if they have a reason of doing this to her.

"She turned down a reward that was right for killing and bringing a man to justice!" Said a woman from the crowd.

Zoiy felt like she was about to crumble being there, and then the song she heard two weeks ago came to her reminding of everyone being the same, "I don't want that type of reward! There is a reason why I'm not taking this."

Everyone then sat quiet and confused, her brother went with their mom and dad sitting at one of the benches on the edge of the field.

"I took this type of job to find an old friend, the one that did all of these murders… He did all of this just because everyone mistreated him when he was in school. His Aunt and Uncle didn't understand to help him. They thought telling someone about it will make it better when it didn't, it made things worse. When I and my family moved to Stamford, I saw this boy sad and lonely. I became his best friend, his only friend; thought him being with me would make things better, but I needed to do more for him. I tried to stop him from killing a boy that picked on him. He also cut opened my arm. He thought he killed me running off feeling the sadness and pain. I know… I saw it in his eyes. This is where most of our school shootings come from, kids being picked on or being treated different. There's no need for it! It doesn't matter if they're disabled, handicapped, deaf, blind, fat, thin, short, tall, even gay. We don't need to mistreat them, IN GOD'S EYES!… In God's eyes we're all the same. Even when they make a choice we still don't need to mistreat them… everyone is special."

She walked away from the stand leaving the football field and so did her family. Everyone watched them, stood quiet once again, and then began to clap for her. Zoiy stopped and turned around see them clapping she smiled alone with crying. Knowing they understood her reason, then continued to walk with her brother driving her back to her house.

Frank ran after her telling her to wait up. He asked her if she can come back to work for him. She said, "No thanks. I'll just go back to my home town to work there doing the same job like I did here."

He then told her he will then do a transfer for her. She said thank you and Frank told her his really going to miss her then shook his hand telling him good bye.

Zoiy and her brother stopped by the cemetery at Christopher's grave seeing it covered in flowers, then she looked at the ring her brother gave her ten years ago. She took it off looking at the inside seeing the word 'Love' then put it in the dirt.

"This was mine for along time, now I want you to have it to show you my love for you."

After she got up, she looked at the grave one last time then went to the car with her brother waiting for her.

"He knows you love him so much."

"I know, I wish it didn't had to come to this."

"We all do sis, we all do."

A month later, Zoiy work in the town where she first met Christopher solving a lot of crimes. While her mom and dad stayed near town and her brother in Anson being a mechanic.

Just about every day, Zoiy goes to the park to watch kids play at the playground and write in her diary. On that day, she saw a boy upset and alone she was about to go to him when then saw a girl go up to him wanting to be his friend. Seeing this reminding of her with Christopher. She seat back down and wrote a paragraph in her diary:

Now I see I'm not the only one that helps people with being different. More are helping as well, but I see the world still the same. I think it doesn't matter. As long there are good people in it. I don't need to work hard as I am now I still miss Christopher, but as long I keep him in my heart always and forever.

Jan. 20, 2012

She then heard Christopher's voice calling her name and saw a hand at the front of her diary. She looked up and saw him smiling at her, she took his hand feeling his warmth touch as she walked with him around the park, then her childhood come along making her feel like a kid with Christopher all those ago, those good memories and a sunset as she watched it go down. She looked at Christopher and he looked at Zoiy smiling at each other then they kissed. Having this moment, she knows he will be there always.

Before it was Writing

This story is almost like me when I was young. Picked on, no friends at first, but later on it got better with having friends. Throughout my school years my thoughts of hurting someone was very disturbing. Snapping, throwing, or hitting a wall was sometimes my way of getting them to leave me alone, but seeing adults helping me out as well made me overcome this issue. Now I'm older I no longer have to worry about that, but I do help others that have to deal with this as well. I sometimes think I might go to that point again, but my Fiancé is helping me a lot now, more then I see with my family. That word different means nothing to me anymore.

April 7, 2011